Jet and his friends were  soccer when Jet's wrist-phone rang. His cousin Zerk was calling him from far away . . . VERY far away. He was calling from Bortron 7, Jet's home planet!

"I have to write about Earth for school," Zerk said. "When was the first time an Earth person landed on Borton 7?"

Jet didn't know the answer. So he asked a friend.

"Mindy, do you know when the first Earthie landed on Bortron 7?"

Mindy replied, "No one from Earth has ever been to Bortron 7."

"The only place we've been to outside of Earth is the moon," she added.

Jet wasn't sure that was right.

Zerk said, "Thanks for the information, Girl from Earth! Bye!"

Then he hung up.

Jet then asked Sydney and Sean.

"When did the first Earthie land on Bortron 7?" Jet asked. "Long ago, right?"

Sydney answered, "Earthies have never been to Bortron 7. We've only been to the moon."

Mindy smiled. "Told you, Jet!"

"When the first Earthies went to the moon, it was a huge deal," Sean said.
"Yes, millions and millions of people on Earth watched it on television," Sydney added.
Sean pulled out his Neil Armstrong action figure and told the story.

"The year was 1969," Sean said.
"Wow! That was about fifty years ago!" Sydney exclaimed.
Sean then said, "Three brave astronauts flew into space." He held up his Neil Armstrong action figure. "Neil Armstrong was one of them. When they got there, two of them walked on the moon!"

"Wow, Sean, you know a lot about this," Jet gushed.

"That's because I love it!" Sean said. "I want to be a space explorer."

Jet wanted to learn more, so he called up his computer friend, FACE 9000.

FACE 9000 appeared in the air.
"FACE 9000, ready to assist you!"
he said.
Jet asked, "Face, could you show us
when the first Earth people walked
on the moon?"
"Of course!" FACE 9000 said.
Sean talked as the computer showed
a video.

"The first person to walk on the
moon was Neil Armstrong," Sean
said, waving his action figure
proudly.
Sean pretended to be the first
astronaut walking on the moon.
"Mindy, you can pretend to be Buzz
Aldrin, the second person to walk
on the moon."

"I'm Buzz Aldrin! I'm walking on the moon!" Mindy yelled.

Sydney got a cool idea.

"We could act out the moon landing!" she said. "We could pretend to be the astronauts."

"What fun!" Jet said. "I bet my mom would really take us to the moon!"

Mindy said, "Wait. I can't go to the real moon. I'm not supposed to go past Jet's yard."

Sydney said, "Don't worry, Mindy. We'll find a job for you on Earth."

Jet then asked if the astronauts used a saucer to zoom to the moon. "Actually, Jet, the astronauts took a huge rocket," Sean explained. FACE 9000 showed them a picture of the tall rocket that took the astronauts to the moon. "Whoa!" the kids shouted.

Sydney said the trip to the moon
took three days.
"THREE DAYS!" Jet said, shocked.
"It takes my family three Earth
MINUTES to get to the moon."

The whole team was very excited.
"Is everyone ready?" Sydney asked.
"Let's start our pretend mission to
the moon!"
"Let's do it!" they all shouted.
"Excelsior!"

Jet's mother said, "Ready to launch!" Sydney told Mindy and Jet's father their jobs.

"You are mission control," Sydney said.

"I'm the boss!" Mindy shouted. "I do the countdown, I say, 'Blastoff!' and I tell you when to land."

Sydney handed Mindy a walkie-talkie. Mindy smiled at Jet's dad. "Mr. Carrot and I can handle this job," she said.

Jet's father gave Mindy a salute and said, "I agree, boss!"

"It's go time!" Sean announced. Jet, Sean, and Sydney walked onto the saucer, pretending to be the three astronauts from the 1969 *Apollo 11* moon mission.

"We could use a space pet," Jet said. Sunspot then ran, rolled, and flipped his way into the saucer.

On the spaceship, Sydney said, "Let's all lie down for the mission, just like the astronauts did back then."

Then Sydney used the walkie-talkie to call Mindy.

"Mission Control Mindy, come in, can you hear me? Time to count down."

"Roger, copy that!" Mindy said.
"Ten . . . nine . . . eight . . . seven . . .
six . . . five . . . four . . . three . . .
two . . . one! Blastoff!"

Jet's family saucer zoomed into
space. "I love pretending to be an
Earth astronaut!" Jet said.
"Me too!" said Sean. "I'll try to stay
calm."

Soon they were so high in space that they could see the whole planet Earth. "I never get tired of seeing Earth," Sean said.

Jet agreed. "It is a really beautiful planet. And I've seen a lot of them with my family."

In space there is practically no gravity, so Jet took off his seat belt and floated. "Woo-hoo! We're almost at the moon," he said.

Jet's mother pointed out the window. "There's Earth's moon!" she said.

"Yay!" the kids cheered.

Sean added, "The real *Apollo 11* slowed down above the moon before it landed."

Sean said, "When Astronaut Neil Armstrong landed on the moon, he said, 'The Eagle has landed!' Their lunar lander was named the Eagle."

"Isn't an eagle a kind of lizard?" Jet asked.

"No," Sydney chuckled. "It's a kind of bird."

"Oh, that makes more sense," said Jet.

Back on Earth, Mindy spoke into the walkie-talkie.
"Mission Control Mindy says you have permission to land on the moon," she said.

Jet's mother landed the saucer on the moon.

"Woo-hoo!" the kids cheered. "The Eagle has landed!"

Back on Earth, Mindy and Jet's father were very happy too.

"Yay! The Eagle has landed!" they shouted.

Sean stepped off the spaceship. He remembered reading that Neil Armstrong said, "That's one small step for man, one giant leap for mankind."

So Sean said, "This is one small step for kids . . . and one gigantic leap for everyone everywhere!"

Everyone followed Sean and jumped around on the moon.
"Yes!" Jet cheered.

Jet's mom took a funny photo for Mindy.
"Best mission to the moon ever!"
Jet said.
Everyone agreed!

Read on to learn some far-out facts about astronauts, the moon, and space!

Did you know there are many different names for space explorers?

- **Astronaut** comes from the Greek words *astron*, meaning star, and *nautes,* meaning sailor. Astronaut is the name used for anyone who travels into space on a NASA (National Aeronautics and Space Administration) or US spacecraft.

- **Cosmonaut** comes from the Greek words *kosmos*, meaning universe, and *nautes*, meaning sailor, and is used by Russian space explorers.

- **Taikonauts** (say: TIE-CO-NOTS) is a term used for Chinese space explorers, and comes from the Chinese word *taikong*, meaning space, and the Greek word *nautes*, meaning sailor.

Do you want to become an astronaut for NASA?

1. The first step is to study hard and do well in school. All astronauts must have a degree in a STEM subject. STEM stands for science, technology, engineering, and math. A degree is something you earn by passing all of your exams and graduating college.

2. The second step is to stay in good physical shape. Astronauts must pass very difficult physical tests to get into the astronaut training program.

3. The third step is to have some sort of work experience connected to the job you would like, such as training as a pilot.

Learn about the first astronauts to land on the moon!

Neil A. Armstrong was born on August 5, 1930, in Wapakoneta, Ohio. While at NASA, he worked as a pilot, an engineer, an administrator, and finally as an astronaut. In 1969, he was named the commander of *Apollo 11* and became the first person to walk on the moon!

Michael Collins was born in Rome, Italy, on October 31, 1930. After moving to the United States, Collins had to apply to NASA twice before being accepted. He would not give up on his dream of being an astronaut! During the *Apollo 11* mission, he stayed in the moon's orbit, which means the path of an object around a star, planet, or moon, while Armstrong and Aldrin walked on the moon.

Edwin (Buzz) E. Aldrin Jr. was born on January 20, 1930 in Montclair, New Jersey. Aldrin was the first astronaut in NASA with a doctorate degree, and the second man to walk on the moon. Aldrin developed special methods for spacecraft landings on Earth and the moon, some of which are still used today!

Our Moon: By the Numbers

- Earth has only 1 natural satellite: the moon! A satellite is a body or object that orbits a planet.

- Our moon is the fifth largest in the solar system.

- Our moon is 4.5 billion years old!

- Even though it looks close, our moon is around 238,855 miles away from Earth. Almost 30 Earths would fit between the Earth and the moon!

- It would take about 4 moons to fill Earth!

- The moon orbits the Earth every 27.3 days.

- We only see about 50–60 percent of the moon at any given time. We never see the entire moon because of the way it orbits Earth.

- The average temperature of the moon during the day is 260 degrees Fahrenheit and -280 degrees Fahrenheit at night—talk about super-hot and super-cold!
- The moon is moving away from the Earth at a rate of about 1 inch per year.

Other Moon Facts

- There are around 158 moons in our solar system.
- Of all the moons, ours is the only one without a proper name. This is because no one knew there were other moons until 1610.
- Mercury and Venus are the only planets without moons due to their proximity, or closeness, to the sun.
- Ganymede (say: GAN-E-MEED) is the largest moon in the solar system and orbits around the planet Jupiter.
- Titan, which orbits the planet Saturn, is the only moon in the solar system with a thick atmosphere. Atmosphere is gas or air that surrounds a planet.
- Not all moons are circular like ours— some of them are lumpy!